The Adventures of Onyx
and
The Angels in the Air

by Tyler Benson

Ensign Benson Books LLC

This book was expertly produced by Book Bridge Press.
www.bookbridgepress.com

book bridge press℠

In memory of the men and women
of the United States Coast Guard who have made
the ultimate sacrifice "so others may live."

In honor of today's men and women
of the United States Coast Guard who risk their lives
every day to serve, protect, and save lives.

—Tyler

"It's good to be back!" Hogan said to Onyx as they looked up at the Mackinac Bridge. "Nothing beats helicopter operations with Air Station Traverse City in the Straits of Mackinac."

"Hogan and Onyx!" Dean shouted. "Get your heads out of the clouds and back on this boat! I have the helo in sight."

"Roger that, Dean!" Hogan said. Onyx barked in agreement.

"Attention to detail my shipmates. Attention to detail," Evans said. "Helo ops require the maximum focus." Evans looked at their newest crewman, Sellers. "You ready for this?"

"Let's find out," Sellers replied.

"Good," Evans said. "We are ready on deck, Dean. Let's get this adventure started!"

Dean moved the motor lifeboat into place.

The helicopter made its approach, hovering above the motor lifeboat. The rotors of the helicopter whistled loudly. Suddenly a line was dropped from the helicopter to the stern. Onyx stood alert and kept her eyes on the crew.

"That's the trail line!" Evans yelled over the wind and spray. "Pull that line in! It's attached to the basket."

Sellers and Hogan began to pull the line in, bringing the basket from the helicopter down to the motor lifeboat. As the basket got closer to the stern, Hogan reached out to grab it.

"Don't touch it!" Evans said, slapping Hogan's arm away. "Static charge. Do you want to get electrocuted?" Evans pointed to the blades of the helicopter. "Static electricity created by the helicopter flows through that basket. Let it touch the boat first and not you, unless you want to get hurt!"

The rescue basket landed on the boat safely. Onyx remained alert.

The helicopter pilot's voice came over the radio. Dean spoke to the pilot, then told the crew, "You're never going to believe this! The pilot recognized our miracle dog and is inviting her for a ride around the Straits of Mackinac! What do you think, girl?"

Onyx barked back to Dean and wagged her tail.

"Hogan!" Dean said. "Go with our girl. Make sure Onyx gets safely up to the helicopter."

"With pleasure!" Hogan said. He climbed into the basket as Sellers picked Onyx up and placed her into Hogan's arms.

Hogan looked at Onyx. "This is where you and I first started," he told her. "In this very spot. Are you ready for another adventure?"

Onyx barked excitedly as the basket lifted toward the helicopter.

When the basket reached the helicopter's cabin door, Onyx and Hogan were met by the flight mechanic and the rescue swimmer. Onyx whimpered in pain from the loud whistle of the helicopter blades. It hurt her sensitive ears. "I am Shaw!" the flight mech yelled over the loud helicopter rotors. "And this is Sinclair!" he said, pointing to the rescue swimmer. "It's nice to meet you!"

Shaw placed headsets on Onyx and Hogan. They silenced the loud helicopter blades. "There, now we don't have to yell," Sinclair said as he petted Onyx.

Suddenly the pilot came over the radio. "We're being diverted to save two people on a capsized sailboat by White Shoals. There is no time to put our new passengers back on the motor lifeboat. We need to go now!"

Shaw slammed the helicopter door shut. "Hold on!" Sinclair said to Onyx and Hogan.

The helicopter flew quickly between the two towers of the Mackinac Bridge and over Lake Michigan. In no time they were soon hovering above White Shoals. Shaw pulled the helicopter door open. Onyx and Hogan looked down. The blue hull of a capsized sailboat could be seen near White Shoal Light.

Sinclair pointed to the sailboat. "I see two people!" he said. "I am going in!"

Onyx watched as Sinclair moved to the edge of the door and looked down. Onyx tried to move closer for a better look, but Hogan pulled her back. Sinclair put his gear on and took a deep breath. He pulled his headset off and secured his hood and helmet. Shaw patted him on the back. Sinclair gave a thumbs up. He looked at Onyx and Hogan. Over the whistle and the wind in the cabin, he mouthed the words, "So others may live!" Then he leaped out of the helicopter, free-falling fifteen feet into Lake Michigan.

Sinclair splashed down into the water and the crew lost sight of him. Then he suddenly burst out of the water and gave a thumbs up, signaling he was okay. Sinclair swam for the capsized sailboat with all his might. As he reached the sailboat, he discovered a woman unconscious and tangled in the lines of the boat. A young girl was on top of the capsized sailboat, crying. She screamed to the rescue swimmer to help her and her mother.

Sinclair climbed on the hull. The girl looked at Sinclair and yelled over the helicopter's wind and spray, "Are you an angel from the air?"

Sinclair grabbed her hand and said, "No. I am a United States Coast Guard rescue swimmer, and I am here to save you and your mother!"

The mother was really hurt, and Sinclair began to untangle her from the sailboat's lines. He radioed up to the helicopter.

Over the headset Onyx and Hogan could hear Sinclair and the pilot talking. Then the pilot asked Hogan if he was an emergency medical technician. "I am," Hogan said, "and I'm ready to help!"

The pilot radioed back to Sinclair and said, "We have a plan!"

Sinclair looked at the frightened girl. "Your mother needs our help immediately," he said. "I have to get her up to the helicopter first for medical attention. I promise I will come back for you!"

Shaw lowered the rescue sling. Sinclair clipped in and secured the mother. He embraced her to prepare for the lift. The young girl grabbed Sinclair and cried, "Please don't leave me." He looked into her eyes and said, "I'll be back for you. I promise."

Onyx watched from the helicopter. She pressed her ears forward and looked down at the water with wide eyes. Tough choices were being made. The crew was nervous, and the little girl was afraid. As Shaw raised Sinclair and the mother off the hull, Onyx leaped out of the helicopter.

Onyx splashed down into the water, surfaced, and swam for the capsized sailboat. The girl helped Onyx out of the water and hugged her tight. Onyx could sense that the little girl was no longer afraid. Onyx looked up to the helicopter. Sinclair transferred the mother to Hogan and Shaw for medical attention. Then he lowered back down to the sailboat to save the young girl, to save Onyx, to fulfill his promise.

Sinclair touched down on the capsized boat. He secured the girl in the rescue sling and grabbed Onyx. "You came back!" the girl cried. "Hold on!" Sinclair said, giving a thumbs up to Shaw. Onyx, the young girl, and Sinclair lifted back up toward the helicopter and the Angels in the Air.

As they reached the door of the helicopter, Shaw quickly pulled them to safety. He slammed the door shut and said to the pilot, "All aboard. All secure. Let's head for Station St. Ignace!"

The pilot said to the flight crew, "Let's go!"

When the helicopter landed at Station St. Ignace, Shaw wasted no time and threw the door open. The mother was quickly transferred to an awaiting ambulance.

The girl looked at Sinclair and said, "Thank you for saving us."

Sinclair took her hand and asked, "What is your name?"

"Molly. And I want to be a rescue swimmer like you. I want to be an Angel in the Air."

Sinclair smiled as he helped Molly into the ambulance next to her mother. Then he shut the doors and knocked to signal to the driver that all was secured. The ambulance turned its lights on and sped away through Station St. Ignace's front gates toward the hospital.

The helicopter powered down, and the pilots stepped out onto the helicopter pad and looked at the crew. Hogan and Onyx walked up to the lead pilot. Hogan saluted and Onyx stood at attention. "Thank you for the ride-along. Thank you for the adventure, sir!"

The lead pilot saluted back and said, "Sir? You mean ma'am," as she took off her helmet.

They couldn't believe who it was. "Pelkey!" Hogan exclaimed. Onyx barked with excitement to see Pelkey.

"I am back!" Pelkey said. "While my girl Onyx and the Guardians of the Straits were fighting the falls in Buffalo, I was at flight school learning how to fly!"

Hogan shook Pelkey's hand and said, "This is such a surprise, ma'am!"

"It's good to be home," she said. Pelkey looked out over the Straits of Mackinac. "It's good to have another adventure with Onyx and the Angels in the Air."

GREAT LAKES AUTHOR **Tyler Benson** is from St. Louis, Michigan. He has served in the United States Coast Guard for more than a decade in St. Ignace, Michigan. He began writing short stories about his search and rescue adventures in the Coast Guard to educate his three young daughters about what Daddy does when he goes on duty for 48 hours at a time. He wanted them to learn the importance of service to their country

and helping those in need. To help them better understand his job, Tyler wrote the stories featuring his station's morale dog, Onyx. These stories soon evolved into a dream—to publish a book series that would serve as a tribute and a way to bring recognition to all who serve or have served in the United States Coast Guard.

The Angels in the Air is Tyler's fourth book in the successful Adventures of Onyx series. Let the adventures continue!

www.adventuresofonyx.com